Other Selected Books by Mark Leslie

Short Story Collections

Novels

Non-Fiction

SNOWMAN SHIVERS
DARK HUMOR SNOWMAN TALES

Mark Leslie

SNOWMAN SHIVERS
DARK HUMOR SNOWMAN TALES

Mark Leslie

DEDICATION

*For Alexander, my son, who brings back the joy,
wonder, and thrill of having fun in the snow.*

TABLE OF CONTENTS

ABOUT THE PRINT EDITION

This 2021 print edition of the original digital chapbook has been updated to include a few additional notes, revisions to the stories, artwork and behind the story notes as well as a brief look at the history of snowmen.

The additional content was partially intended to bring extra value to anybody purchasing the print-book copy (as the eBook was always intended to be a free read – and has remained free on most eBook retailers – with the exception of some sites that don't allow free books; in which case it'll be listed at 99 cents USD), and partially to enhance the length required for effective print binding.

IT SNOWED LAST NIGHT

A Note from the Author

I'll be entirely honest here; when I was little, I had never been particularly frightened of snowmen.

I'm not sure why. Because my whole life I've been afraid of the monster under my bed, the one hiding in my closet and all the ghosts and ghouls that I know lurk within the shadows wherever I roam around after dark.

But snowman never really gave me the creeps.

Despite the fact that, when you think about them, snowmen can be rather scary. I mean, look at how they are constructed. What kind of a life is that?

A body made of three balls of packed snow piled atop one another? A pair of broken tree branch sticks for arms

Not to mention those dark black eyes of coal.

But even though I've never been frightened of snowmen I've written about them – and seem to have been fascinated with the basic idea of a snowman actually coming to life, like in the classic Christmas carol that children joyfully sing each year; but in my imagination it's not always quite as joyful and magical an experience as in the song.

Perhaps my fascination with snowmen comes from growing up in a more northerly part of Canada (I grew up in Levack, a small town about an hour's drive north of Sudbury, Ontario – and we had REAL winters there, not the pseudo winters that I now experience in Southern Ontario. Winters up north were long; the snow was plentiful. I truly enjoyed cavorting in the snow for afternoons and evenings after school that seemed to last forever.

When I was young, snowmen were just a part of the natural winter wonderland snowscape I cherished.

Now, though, I tend to throw a cautious glance over my shoulder whenever I pass once, particularly when walking down a dark, deserted street . . .

Mark Leslie
April 2021

Snowman eating child - Levack, Ontario January 2015
Used in the design of this book's cover
Photo by Mark Leslie Lefebvre

THAT OLD SILK HAT THEY FOUND

A cool wind kisses me.

Little by little the sensation rises, becomes more real. The soft light breeze becomes an intense, encompassing cold. But the cold doesn't hurt me — it soothes me. It feels good, comfortable.

Relaxed in the darkness, I realize that my eyes are closed. What am I saying? I realize, for the first time, that I have eyes.

I open my eyes to see the world through some sort of charcoal grey lens. But despite the blurry grey haze I can make out a white landscape and figures moving in the distance. Running and cavorting, their shouts are muffled. I can barely hear them.

I can barely see, I can barely hear.

But I do have life.

It's an incredible feeling — almost overwhelming.

I don't really understand who or what I am, but having life feels good. Knowing that I exist and that I can sense and feel is wonderful.

I try to move, but I can't. I look down.

No!

I don't have legs — just this big round mass.

I look to my sides. My arms are mere sticks. They flail uselessly in the wind.

Who created me? Who gave me this cruel life? Was it those kids who frolic so joyfully in the snow? It must have been. They are the only other ones here. Can't they see what a horrid creature they have conjured? Can't they tell what a torture this life is that they have given me?

"Hey!"

A deep voice calls to me. Who is it that addresses me? Certainly not the children, for they are still ignoring me. The voice sounds much different, much clearer and closer than the voices of the children. My eyes scan the landscape.

"Hey, you! Newcomer!"

Finally, my eyes spot the owner of the voice. He is one like me, off to my left. I can tell he is like me because instead of legs and feet, his bottom is a large white mass of snow. He is built like three large balls stacked upon one another. There is a scarf wrapped around his neck. He has dark lumps for eyes, a carrot nose, two sticks like mine, bobbing in the wind, and several tiny stones in a line which form a horridly ironic grin.

I try to respond, but I cannot make a sound.

"Don't even try to speak. You can't. They didn't give you a mouth," the other one says.

They didn't give me a mouth? Feeble arms, no legs, no mouth. What evil creatures they must be! Why even bother to give me life, then?

"Welcome to the world, Frosty."

Frosty? Is that my name? Did they at least give me a name? I wonder, what is the name of my companion?

"In case you're wondering, my name's Frosty too. For the most part, even if they do name us, we're all called Frosty at one time or another. I guess it's supposed to be a funny name for a snowman. But for the sake of personality, you can call me Oldtimer. I've been alive for ages now. Can you believe that I'm four weeks old? Geez, where does the time go?

"Well, since you're new, I'll give you the low-down. God, it's so good to be able to talk to someone again. Do you know that I've been alone now for almost two weeks?"

Just then, a child runs up to Oldtimer. "Hey now!" Oldtimer says. "Get your paws off of me!" But the child laughs and grabs at the nose.

"YAAAAAAAAARGHHHH!" Oldtimer's scream cuts through my head. I can almost feel his pain as the child wrenches the nose free and runs, laughing, through the snow. Another child, upset, chases after him, determined to get the carrot back.

Oldtimer is quiet for a moment. I wonder if he's okay. I wonder if he's still alive.

I wonder if they create us just to torture us.

"Stupid little brat!" Oldtimer says in a low moan. The anguish is clear in his voice. "I'm okay, now. It hurts, but not so bad as I imagine it was for Sammy."

Sammy? Who is Sammy?

"Sammy was my last companion. He stood not four feet from where you now are. And if you think I'm old, he'd been around from the beginning of time. He was the one who explained to me all about what being a snowman means. Do you want to hear it?

"Well, since you can't speak, then you can't object and you're going to have to hear it.

"If you haven't already guessed, humans created us. We are created merely for their pleasure. From what little I have learned of humans, they do this quite often. They create all kinds of creatures merely to use them as they see fit — and to dispose of in a likewise manner. Sammy told me stories of them breeding creatures merely to eat or to keep as what are called pets. I guess that we're like pets. Except, of course, we can't do much more than stand here. At least their other pets have the freedom to roam around. See this yellow stain at the bottom of my right side? It's a little gift from one of their pets called Spike.

"But what nerve, eh? What gall. To automatically assume ownership of another species — to create another being and then to destroy it for their own pleasure."

Oldtimer is silent again. And it is then that the child who took off after the one with the carrot returns, triumphantly holding the carrot up high. She returns to Oldtimer and sinks the carrot into his face.

He grunts as she does this.

Then the girl turns and looks across at me. She frowns, turning her head to the side. She mutters something and walks forward.

I've never known such fear, such dread. She's coming at me and I can't do anything about it. Trying desperately to cringe and shrink back, I close my eyes and wish I could at least scream.

Her finger sinks into the front of my face. I can feel a painful warmth tearing into me. It becomes a burning sensation — incredibly intense. I feel as if my head is going to explore in a bright burst of white light.

A scream, louder than the one Oldtimer made a few minutes ago, rings in my head. It goes on and on, then Oldtimer yells. "For Pete's sake, cut it out, will you?"

The screaming is coming from me?

I try to stop the noise and sure enough, it stops. I open my eyes to find the little girl smiling up at me. She wasn't hurting me intentionally — she was melting me a mouth.

"Thank you," I say to her, but she is oblivious. She begins dancing around me and singing, but it makes no sense. She sings about a jolly, happy snowman. Her song confuses me. How the hell can a snowman be jolly?

"Hey," I say to Oldtimer.

"So now you have a mouth. I know it must have hurt like a bugger, but it's good you can talk. Sammy said that it was important for us to be able to talk."

"Why is that? I ask.

"Because we have a legacy to pass along. We are created and then can do nothing about our existence. But if we can speak, then at least we can pass along stories to each other. So we have an oral tradition to uphold. We pass along speculative tales of what's to come."

Of what's to come? What is he talking about?

I have to ask: "What happened to Sammy?"

"He was torn apart. Tortured. Smashed to pieces by a gang of kids. It was horrible, watching them do it, listening to his screams. It was, so far, the worst experience I've ever faced — except, of course, for being completely alone these past two weeks."

A muffled yell cuts through Oldtimer's speech. I look to see a group of kids approaching. The girl dancing around me runs in the opposite direction and as the gang nears, I recognize the leader as the one who pulled Oldtimer's nose off.

"Here it comes," Oldtimer says. "Finally, our salvation."

"Our salvation? What are you talking about?"

The first of the kids arrives, kicking a large chunk of snow from Oldtimer. A second kid starts throwing punches. A third kid tears into him, ripping away huge chunks. All along, Oldtimer wails and screams.

It's more terrible than he described.

There is nothing I can do. I look about and see, in the direction the girl ran, a large group of kids coming.

"Hey Oldtimer!" I yell. "Hang in there. It looks like help is on the way."

He moans. "Help? No. No. I'm almost . . . free."

"What the hell are you talking about?"

Punches and kicks send snow flying in all directions. Oldtimer speaks between screams, moans and grunts. "If . . . you think . . . this . . . is a bad way . . . to die," he cuts off for a moment, his voice drowned in an anguished wallow.

"What? What could be worse?"

I can barely see him now through the flailing arms and legs. The little girl and her gang are getting closer, yelling something. Will they arrive in time to save my friend?

"Before he died . . . Sammy told me . . . about, " another wail, "the apocalypse."

"The apocalypse?"

"Yes. The slowest . . . most painful death . . . you can imagine . . . when everything . . . melts. They call it . . . spring. Just pray . . .that you're not around," there is a long pause as he fights to summon up his last words, "when . . . spring comes."

The second gang of kids arrive and quickly chase the others off with a barrage of snowballs and yells. But it is too late. When they clear the area I can see Oldtimer. He is nothing now but a pile of snow with a few broken sticks, some stones and a scarf.

He has found his salvation.

The kids fuss over the pile of snow and then turn their attention to me, long enough to add Oldtimer's scarf to my neck. They chat for a bit and then leave me to solitude.

Time passes. I can't even cry.

My eyes cast fervently across the fields of snow. My fear is that I'll spot some children off in the distance be-ginning the ritual of building another snowman. I don't think I could even bear to watch.

I yearn for the mean kids to return. To smash me down the way they destroyed Oldtimer. At least it was quick. I'm remembering when the little girl melted me a mouth and how the burning sensation was the worst I had ever felt. I don't think I can even imagine what it will be like when spring comes and I slowly melt down to nothing.

Now, all I can do is sit here and wait.

And wonder if the torture of melting will be much worse than the agony of knowing now that spring is inevitable.

"Oldtimer"
Original Art by Nikolette Jones
www.nikolettejonesart.ca

IDES OF MARCH

A cruel, unavoidable empathy has overcome me today.

It had been an otherwise typical day in the middle of March. Spring was coming in like a lamb, and I had the radio deejay repeatedly reminding me of it all morning. Repetitive as his ramblings were, the fact that I was sitting at my desk in the front window and was thus witness to the weather made it all the more redundant.

But I needed the deejay's company; to keep me sane.

I'd been there at the desk near the window all morning on self-appointed sick leave. No, I wasn't ill, but I did have to fill out the tax forms for my wife and I, and if neither of us got on the ball, they'd never get done. On second thought, maybe I was sick. Why else would I volunteer for such a task?

So I sat there, playing with numbers, feeling the warm sun on my face with the easy listening radio station filtering old top 40 tunes to my mind. The temperature outside was just above zero, I could tell, for the previously icy sidewalks were now infested with puddles.

The warm temperature left the remaining snow wet and sticky. The neighbor's eight year old boy, Charlie

Fung, was putting the finishing touches on what would probably be his last snowman of the year.

Everything was normal. Everything was fine. And except for the grueling hours and triplicate form headaches that lay ahead of me, it was a pleasant day.

Then this black truck, a Range Rover, I believe, appeared from around the corner of our street and Fifth Avenue and swerved dramatically, taking a long wide turn into the double driveway that we shared with the Fungs.

Two figures sat in the cab, but it was hard to see them through the glare of the sun on the windshield. I was certain that they were drunk, or at least the driver was, the way he'd maneuvered the vehicle. That upset me. I mean, it was barely noon, and already drunk drivers were on the road, endangering lives. I'd never seen this truck before and wondered what connection these yahoos might have with the Fungs, who were very conservative, peaceful and quiet neighbors.

Both figures stumbled out of the truck and confirmed my suspicions about their drunkenness. Their fashion sense wasn't much better. They were large, overweight, and dressed in similar beige full length overcoats, blue baggy ski pants and wool hats with long, floppy brims that kept their faces in shadow.

Together, they lurched toward Charlie, who was looking up at them from his recently created masterpiece. The driver was the first to reach the boy and as he approached, he grabbed Charlie by the shoulder and threw him to the snow.

I sprang from my desk and ran back through the living room, into the kitchen and down the steps to the front door. When I burst into the front yard, Charlie was sitting in the snow, crying silently, and the two men were carrying away the snowman.

When Charlie saw me, he started to wail out loud, and I rushed over to see if he was all right.

"The pushed me!" He bawled. "They pushed me! They pushed me!" He continually repeated this phrase, louder and louder. For an obscure moment I wondered if he held any relation to the deejay who'd been keeping me company all morning with his repetitive and redundant words.

Assured that Charlie wasn't hurt, just scared, I looked up to see that the two strangers were putting Charlie's snowman into the back of the truck where five other snowman sat.

I wouldn't be surprised if my jaw hit the snow as I stood there watching.

Stealing snowmen from children?

What kind of mentally unbalanced people was I dealing with here? Our world was getting more and more stupid each passing day.

I walked over to the strangers. "Hey buddy," I said, putting my hand on the driver's shoulder from behind. "What's the big ide . . ."

I stopped.

His shoulder was cold and soft, and my hand mashed down into it easily.

He turned to face me, staring at me with big black eyes. No, they weren't eyes.

They were chunks of coal.

And his flesh was pale white, nothing more than snow. He was sweating profusely. No, not sweating. Melting. His face was melting, and it continued to change its shape before me, the melting water running down his slushy face, the carrot nose beginning to sag.

He said something to me. Or at least he tried to, for his melting face seemed without a mouth. It came out as a mumbled warning of some kind.

Then he pushed me — hard. In the face. His hand was wet and slushy. There was an immediate bitter-cold sensation in my mouth and on my tongue — not unlike a shot of Novocain from the dentist — and I realized I must have eaten a couple of his fingers. The numbing sensation immediately dribbled down the back of my throat.

I stumbled, back, numb, dumbfounded, and fell on my ass.

I sat there in the snow, quiet and wide eyed the way Charlie had been when I first came out of the house, and watched them clamber into the cab again. The truck pulled out of the driveway, backed into a telephone post across the street and then went forward, down to the end of the street, and disappeared around the corner.

I'm not sure where these twisted snowmen came from.

But I certainly know where they're heading.

North.

Although I couldn't at first make out the mumbled word the driver had said to me, I think I've figured it out.

It was a desperate, guttural moan, a warning, spoken the same rushed way that way Chicken Little must have bleated, "The sky is falling! The sky is falling!" in the classic Henny Penny tale.

The word I believe the snowman was trying to utter was: Spring.

Spring.

Nothing more than a season to us. But to a snowman, it was the end of the world.

Whoever they were, however they came to exist, Frosty and his friend were heading north and taking as many of their own kind with them as they could gather, the way that birds migrate south for the winter. They were running from the apocalyptic season of spring.

I wondered if they would make it.

Then, shortly after I escorted Charlie to his home and explained the situation to his parents — leaving out the fact that the thieves were snowmen themselves — I came back inside and took my place at the window.

Sitting here in the window again, the sunlight on my face, sweat running down my brow, I begin to wonder something else.

Spring is coming in like a lamb, a soft mild day. But ever since I swallowed the snow flesh of the animate snowman, the numbness has continued to spread throughout my insides. And I've become more and more uncomfortable in the heat. I keep checking the temperature because it feels like one hundred degrees — but it's really only plus three.

I look down at my sweat, at the pools of thick fleshy sweat that has dripped onto my desk, onto the tax forms.

And I wonder if I would be able to find them again.

I wonder if they'd take me with them.

The taxes, Charlie, my wife, none of them seem important to me now.

I'd just like to head north, find a deserted field, and spend the rest of my days standing there, basking in the freezing arctic temperatures.

DUSTING OFF THE SNOW

Behind the Shivers

If you don't like getting the story behind the story or to "see the strings" behind the play and absolutely never watch the special features on a DVD where you can listen to commentary by the director, actors, writers, etc., then I suggest that you stop here. I doubt you'd enjoy what is about to come.

But I do want to thank you for coming this far with me. I hope that you enjoyed your experience and didn't mind the fun chilly shivers of these two snowman tales and are curious to check out more of my work. I have several other short stories and a few books available in eBook, print and audio format. *One Hand Screaming*, for example, is a full-sized collection of short fiction of a similar dark and "Twilight Zone" or "Black Mirror" style which also includes these two tales. *Bumps in the Night* and my series of *Nocturnal Screams* collections are, like this, shorter and only contain three or four stories on a theme.

However, if you're one who is willing to walk along with the author and listen to some of the details behind the stories and poems that appear in this collection, then come along with me for a brief jaunt. There's a beautiful blanket of freshly fallen snow on the ground, and the full moon's light is casting a beautiful magical glow. Grab your coat, hat and mitts. Let me bend your ear for a few minutes more.

Just do me a favour and keep your eyes out for any of those silent snowy sentinels we might pass, would you?

That Old Silk Hat They Found
First published in *Strange Wonderland* #1, March 1997

Ides of March
First published in **One Hand Screaming**, October 2004

"That Old Silk Hat They Found" is one of those tales that had been inspired entirely by a previously written story of mine: "Ides of March." It was in the early 1990's when I was living in Ottawa and I heard a radio news blurb about a man somewhere in the southern U.S. who'd been shot by someone who proceeded to steal his snowman.

It was a quick, short news update, but it fascinated me.

I wondered what kind of a person would shoot another person to steal a snowman.

And then it came to me: a person who thought perhaps, that by stealing the snowman and bringing them north to a colder climate, he could help them escape spring and what would be certain death.

It would kind of be like an environmentalist or animal lover risking his life to save a helpless baby seal from needless slaughter.

But that still wasn't enough, I felt, to make it really interesting. So the idea continued to stay warm on a back burner.

A few days later, another idea occurred to me.

What if the "man" who stole the snowman was actually a snowman himself – on a mission to save as many of his kind as possible?

I wrote the story and called it "Ides of March" (March 15th being a date not only thought of as a type of literary D-Day thanks to the warning given to Julius Caesar, but also a time when spring-type weather is likely to intensify – particularly back in the 1990's in Ottawa, which also experienced the type of real winters that I enjoyed in the Sudbury region).

This story was told from the point of view of a middle-aged man doing his taxes. The tale starts as he witnesses, through the window, two burly men in long jackets shoving at the neighbour's kid and stealing his snowman. I liked the tale, but not enough. I wrote it and only half heartedly sent it out to a few markets, then relegated it to my own personal slush pile (yes, in this case the pun is completely intended).

After a short period of time, I considered re-telling one of the premises of the tale.

The thought of associating spring with *The Apocalypse* was still intriguing to me; this time, however, I did it from the snowman's point of view.

As I began to write the tale, I made the snowman a sentient narrator, and the narrator's voice began to take over the story, describing what it was like to wake up and find oneself to be a snowman.

Inspired partly by Frankenstein's monster, who didn't ask to be "born" and partly by wanting to make a statement about the self-imposed God complex of humanity in general, I kept up this train of thought and considered the following questions:

What would it be like to be a snowman?

How would a snowman think and feel about its circumstances?

What would their "life" be like and what would an expected "lifespan" be?

What tales would they tell?

Culturally and anthropologically speaking, what legends of Genesis *and* Armageddon *would they pass along to each other?*

These questions led me to the reasoning that *Spring,* and the cruel humans who selfishly created this "life" were the enemies as the narrator faced his darkest fears.

I'm particularly fond of the title as it calls upon the happy and innocent mystique of the children's song "Frosty the Snowman" and turns on the reader when they encounter what I felt would be a more realistic experience of a snowman coming to life.

After finishing that story, and having it published in the late 1990's I was pleased.

But I wasn't fully satisfied.

My thoughts returned to the idea of someone wanting to steal a snowman.

So I looked at "The Ides of March" and revised the ending, based on having put myself into the POV of the snowman in "That Old Silk Hat . . ." – I determined that it wasn't enough for my narrator to have witnessed this strange event. No. I felt he had to experience the horror himself. Something had to occur in which he didn't just sympathize with the snowmen's plight and fear of spring – he needed to experience it first-hand.

Thus, I re-wrote the tale with the ending it has now. With the narrator fully feeling the terror of knowing he'll melt if he doesn't get to a warmer climate.

When these stories were originally republished in my book *One Hand Screaming* in the fall of 2004, I received many comments from readers about how much they enjoyed "the snowman tales." People still contact me to comment on those two stories.

I've also gone into classrooms and read "That Old Silk Hat They Found" to students – and it's one of my favourite short tales to read at public readings.

The story is available in audio format via a podcast I released called "Prelude to a Scream" – it appears in episode 5.

I had long thought that there's still more snowman tales in me. Thoughts of writing a zombie-like snowman story still kick around, as do images, likely born from reading too many Calvin and Hobbes cartoons, of snowmen learning how to create more of their own kind and amassing a large army.

I did write another snowman story; but the only horror in the tale was that it was a look at teen suicide. The story, "Impression in the Snow" tells the tale of a teenager who is about to end her life when she sees an impossible site. A snowman from her childhood. Yes, that tale does involve a sentient snowman, but it is a decidedly different story; one of angst and, ultimately, of hope. It was published in 2016 in an anthology entitled *Fiction River: Sparks* from WMG Publishing (which is available in print and eBook format) and is a tale I am quite proud of.

I will likely write more snowman stories one day – and I'm pretty sure I'll have just as much fun as I did with these first two snowmen tales.

In any case, thanks for joining me on this walk and one-way chat.

The wind is starting to get cold. I'm sure that, inside there's a hot cup of cider or a warm cup of cocoa waiting.

Hopefully you'll join me on another walk on some other evening.

Until then, thanks for coming along and we'll talk to you soon.

Mark Leslie

A LOOK AT ANTHROPOMORPHIC SNOW SCULTURES

A Brief History of Snowmen

Though I doubt it needs a definition, one might describe a snowman as an anthropomorphic (having human traits or characteristics) snow sculpture. These sculptures, which are usually composed of three large rolled balls of snow stacked upon one another, with the smallest one on the top representing the creature's head, are often built by children in particularly snowy regions of the world.

The most common accessories used to further define these creatures include other objects suck as sticks for arms, rocks (or pieces of coal) for the eyes and mouth as well as representing a vertical row of buttons in the "chest" area, a stick or a carrot for the nose, a winter scarf, a toque or a top hat.

Like the classic cartoon characters of Donald Duck or Winnie the Pooh, snowmen often aren't given pants, or even the representation of pants.

While the actual history of the snowman is unclear, one of the earliest pieces of photographic evidence of a snowman appears in an 1853 photograph from Wales.

The Snowman No. 2 - Mary Dillwyn (Llyfrgell Genedlaethol Cymru / The National Library of Wales from Wales/Cymru)

In his book *The History of the Snowman*, author Bob Eckstein cited illustrations, woodcuts and artistic depictions of snowmen from medieval times. The earliest illustrated appearance of a snowman that he found originated from a 1380 Christian devotional prayer book, called a book of hours.

The marginal illustration appears to be an oddly anti-Semitic rendition of a Jewish snowman melting beside a fire. It appears next to a passage of text that describes the crucifixion of Jesus.

In 1511, snowmen were used as a form of protest in Brussels. During what has been described as the "Winter of Death," a particularly miserable period where bitterly freezing temperatures persisted in the city for many months, the government decided to create a snowman festival to enlighten the spirits of the population.

In response, despondent artistic citizens created boldly graphic caricatures of leaders, and wealthy, prominent citizens; they also littered the city with pornographic sculptures made of snow.

Of course, there were snowman built for positive and romantic reasons as well. The 1934 song "Winter Wonderland" (written by Felix Bernard and Richard B. Smith) often considered a Christmas Carol, because of it's seasonal theme, involves a couple enjoying a snowy landscape and creating a snowman that they name "Parson Brown" and imagine he can marry them right there on the spot.

Perhaps the most well-known snowman song, and the one that is referred to most prominently in "That Old Silk Hat They Found" in this collection, is "Frosty the Snowman," which was written by Walter "Jack" Rollins and Steve Nelson in 1950.

The Frosty song, which was first performed by Gene Autry, was written in response to the huge success of another Autry song the previous year, "Rudolph, The Red-Nosed Reindeer."

In 1950 a short black-and-white 3-minute animated film brought the "Frosty" from this song to life. Featuring an acapella jazzy rendition of the song, it played on the

Chicago based WGN-TV as a regular seasonal favorite, playing as a short featured on various children's shows such as "The Bozo Show," "Garfield Goose," and "Ray Rayner and His Friends."

Rankin/Bass Productions used the voice talents of Jimmie Durante (Narrator), Billy De Wolfe (Professor Hinkle), Paul Frees (Santa), June Foray (Karen), and Jackie Vernon (Frosty) to create a 25-minute color animated television special that endures as an annual favorite of children and adults alike.

Three sequels to the original special were created. *Frosty's Winter Wonderland* (1976), which is related to the song of the same name, involves Frosty getting married. *Rudolph and Frosty's Christmas in July* (1979), which saw Frosty and Rudolph unite in a stop-animation tale, similar to the technique ("Animagic") used for the original *Rudolph the Red-Nosed Reindeer* television special. In 2005, *The Legend of Frosty the Snowman* was released and is only loosely based on the original story and has no connection or narrative mention of the Christmas holiday.

A completely stand-alone story featuring the voice talent of John Goodman as Frosty and Jonathan Winters as the narrator was created in 1992. Entitled *Frosty Returns* it is meant to be a sequel to the original song and is set in an entirely different fictional universe than the other stories.

Apart from the very popular variations of *Frosty the Snowman*, snowmen in popular culture have also appeared in some of these following ways:

- *The Snowman* is an illustrated children's book by UK author Raymond Briggs about a boy who builds a snowman that comes to life and takes him on an adventure to the North Pole.
- Olaf, the snowman character from the 2013 animated film *Frozen* who longs to experience summer. The same film's musical score also includes the song "Do You Want to Build a Snowman?"
- Two decidedly different snowman movies named *Jack Frost*. The first, a 1996 horror/thriller tale about a serial killer who is transformed into a snowman. The second, a 1998 movie in which actor Michael Keaton plays a man who, after a car accident, wakes up as a snowman.
- Multiple different instances of the cartoon boy Calvin from Bill Watterson's *Calvin and Hobbes* cartoon strip creating abnormal, amusing and often darkly humorous snowman sculptures. The 1992 collection of Watterson's cartoons entitled *Attack of the Deranged Mutant Killer Monster Snow Goons* features one of the sequences of Calvin creating a Frankenstein's Monster style version of a snow goon on the cover.
- The imaginative and fun 2005 children's picture book *Snowmen at Night* written by Caralyn Buehner and illustrated by Mark Buehner which explores the games and activities snowmen get up to at night when nobody is watching. It was followed up by the creators with *Snowmen at*

Christmas (2005), *Snowmen All Year (2010)*, *Snowmen at Work* (2012), and *Snowmen at Halloween (2019)*.

- Since 2005, in Anchorage, Alaska, a local resident (Billy Powers) has erected a gigantic snowman called *Snowzilla* on the front yard of his property. In the first year, the snowman, which featured a corncob pipe, a carrot nose, and two beer bottles for eyes, was 16 feet tall. In 2006, it was 22 feet tall. In 2008, the height of the snowman was 25 feet.
- The world's largest snowman on record was of the female variety and was created in 2008 in Maine. In the town of Bethel, the snow-woman created stood 122 feet and 1 inch and was named in honor of the governor at the time, Olympia Snow. The previous record was set in the same town in 1999 for a snowman that stood 113 feet 7 inches and was nicknamed "Angus, King of the Mountain" after the governor of that time named Angus King.
- In London, Ontario, Canada, at University of Western, Ontario (UWO), the smallest recorded "snowman" (in shape at least, if not in structural components) was created in a nano-fabrication in 2016, using roughly 0.9 micron spheres of silica, platinum arms and legs, and an ion beam for the face.

Maybe we like the concept of snowmen having human traits, characteristics, and feelings because they are simplified, less complex representations of ourselves.

As I explored in both of the stories in this collection, they, like us, are only around for a limited time. And, since it's easier to reflect on one's own mortality when looking at something else that is easier to conceptualize (the "lifespan" of a snowman can be seen almost in a glimpse, after all, rather than a typical human life, which spans decades).

In another one of my more recent snowman tales "Impressions in the Snow" which appeared in *Sparks* (Issue 17 of the Fiction River anthology series, this one edited by Rebecca Moesta), my encounter is between a suicidal teenager and a snowman. While it is a dark tale, there is no humor to it; I use their unique relationship to draw out a specific element of humanity as well as to highlight an all too common teen issue. The snowman might be simple, but he is wise in other ways.

We see ourselves in snowmen.

We create ourselves in snowmen.

After all, as anthropomorphic creatures, snowmen are us.

Sources and more information:

https://en.wikipedia.org/wiki/Snowman
https://allthatsinteresting.com/history-of-snowmen

THE SNOWMAN SHIVERS
CHAPBOOK

A Brief History of this chapbook

The snowman shivers chapbook was originally published as an eBook to spotlight a particular theme in my writing.

I am constantly experimenting with various forms and designs using different formats.

For example, the chapbook **Active Reader** was originally a book I slapped together when I was working at the bookstore at McMaster University. We had an *Espresso Book Machine* in the store. (An *Espresso Book Machine*, or *EBM* for short, is a machine not all that much larger than an industrial sized photocopier, that will print and bind a trade paperback right on the spot in about ten or fifteen minutes.)

I was the chief operator and business owner of the *EBM* and I wanted to create a short book to use to test different paper and other factors on the machine. So, instead of printing a 300-page book (which would take a lot longer), I wanted something that was maybe 30 or 40 pages – enough for the spine to catch the glue, but small enough that it wouldn't waste as much paper and ink.

That book turned into an ePub – a digital chapbook – a year or two later as I continued to experiment in the eBook realm (recognizing that eBook size and length could vary even further).

Snowman Shivers was originally created back in 2011 in eBook format. It was listed with a price of $0.00 on all platforms that allowed free eBooks (Amazon doesn't allow that price, and so it is only free in the territories where they have price-matched other retailers – otherwise it might be listed at $0.99). It was meant to be used as a funnel to get people to check out my longer book of short stories, **One Hand Screaming**, which was available in print and eBook format.

The eBook has received plenty of positive reviews and these two snowman stories are the ones that I have received the most emails about from readers.

When I do live readings, "That Old Silk Hat They Found" is one that is a popular audience favorite. It is short enough that I can read the entire tale, and it's funny and gets the best audience reaction. I have read it to both adult and children audiences alike, as it's one of the safer of my tales that I can read to a young audience.

I even revised the subtitle (and the cover) after reading a review that helped me realize I had misrepresented the book.

The original subtitle was *Scary Snowman Tales*.

However, the tales aren't really scary. They're though-provoking and contain dark humor.

And though the original cover image invoked a cold snowy landscape, it didn't even have a snowman on it.

So, I updated it to the more appropriate: **Snowman Shivers:** *Two Short Dark Humor Tales About Snowmen.*

And I also fine-tuned the cover image with a photo I took a few years ago on the street where my mom lives in Levack, Ontario, the hometown where I grew up.

Both the new subtitle and the cover do a better job of informing the potential reader about what they are getting.

This revised eBook is the result of another new test for format as well as an interesting thing that happened in the summer of 2019.

In June 2019, I was doing a book signing at a bookstore in Cambridge, Ontario. For the multi-author event, I had brought in a few of my titles that the store was holding in consignment fashion. One of the print books I'd brought was the 70-page chapbook **Active Reader:** *And Other Cautionary Tales from the Book World* which I have already mentioned. When testing the Draft2Digital Print beta program in 2019, I had to make the page count a minimum of 70 pages. So I added on to the front and back matter for the existing book in order to fill up those pages. One of the things I added was a "Other Selected Books by Mark Leslie" page in the very front.

The bookseller working at the cash desk who had browsed through the books on display near the cash, asked me why I hadn't brought a copy of **Snowman Shivers**, which appeared in the "short story collections" carousel. She mentioned that it had perked her interest.

I explained to her that it was a digital only product, an eBook I had created and intended to give away for free so people could check out my writing, and, hopefully, go on to buy one of my books.

But her question prompted those cogs in my head to kick into gear.

I had created this eBook years earlier and it was a popular one; garnering plenty of positive reception from readers.

So why *didn't* I make a print version of it?

Well, to start, unlike **Active Reader** there were only two stories, and they were both shorter than those other tales. So, it wouldn't just involve a few formatting tweaks and the insertion of a few extra pages.

In order to get the book to the 70 pages needed to generate a print copy via Draft2Digital Print, I would need to add something more.

The only other snowman short story I had written and published (and could feasible re-publish) was one called "Impressions in the Snow" and was about teen suicide. It was a dark tale, and, although the ending is a positive one, it wouldn't fit into "dark humor" in any way, shape, or form.

As I was wondering what I could do, I figured it might be interesting to explore snowmen in popular culture, and maybe even history. After all, since the stories do rely a little on the reader understanding the classic *Frosty the Snowman* song and animated cartoon, it might be fun to explore other snowmen tropes and appearances.

I set about to do a little research and found all kinds of articles and interesting tidbits about snowmen; both world records and other intriguing facts and various snowmen appearances in comics, film, and television.

But, as some creative projects often go, I kept finding ways to enhance and update this book.

In early 2021, when I was getting ready to do a virtual haunted campfire event with the folks from Haunted Walks (Ottawa, Kingston, Toronto), they had asked me to share a compilation of true ghostly and eerie stories from near Sudbury, Ontario, my old stomping grounds. Along with ghost stories, UFO tales, and other unexplainable phenomenon, I included the family-friendly story "That Old Silk Hat They Found."

Because the talk was a virtual event, I needed to submit different images that could be shown while I was reading. (The occasional pop-up image keeps the event less static than just looking at me on a screen while talking or reading).

I reached out to a talented artist friend of mine, Nikolette Jones, and asked if I could commission a piece of art for the reading.

She came up with a black and white sketch images that she sent me after sketching it. I fell in love with it immediately and she kept sending updates on it, adding in the background of the landscape, the trees, and the colors.

Nikolette is a brilliantly talented artist who is easy to work with and I'm thrilled to have her work in this revised print edition of the book.

The black and white images you see in this book don't do her magnificence proper justice. You can see the full colour spectacular version of her artwork on my website at:

www.markleslie.ca/snowmanshivers

And, though this might be the fifth update I've made to the original free eBook story collection, I've continued to have plenty of fun compiling the stories, the tales behind the stories, as well as a brief look at snowmen in general and adding in some more visual elements to make the print version that much more attractive.

And I hope that you enjoyed reading them.

The original cover and subtitle for the eBook
Cover image photo by Greg Roberts

ABOUT THE ARTIST

Nikolette Jones is an artist and teacher with a BEd, located in Alberta, Canada. She finds inspiration in pop culture and literary works and uses a variety of media to create paintings, illustrations and home decor.

She has illustrated the Nikki Knox series of books by Canadian author Shawn Bird, has created multiple commissioned pieces of art for other writers, and is available for additional custom art pieces, private art lessons and paint parties.

Learn more about Nikolette at www.nikolettejonesart.ca.

ABOUT THE AUTHOR

Mark Leslie is a writer, editor and bookseller who was born and grew up in Sudbury, Ontario, spent many years in Ottawa, Ontario and currently lives in Southern Ontario.

A bookselling veteran for more than twenty years, Mark has worked at virtually every type of bookstore, has sat on the Board of Directors for BookNet Canada and also been President of the Canadian Booksellers Association, was the Director of Self-Publishing and Author Relations at Kobo from 2011 to 2017 and is currently Director of Business Development for Draft2Digital. He has given talks across Canada and the United States, in London, Paris and Frankfurt on the bookselling, writing and publishing industry.

You can learn more about Mark and sign up for his newsletter at www.markleslie.ca.

Other Books by Mark Leslie

Canadian Werewolf

This Time Around (Prequel / Short Story)

A Canadian Werewolf in New York

Stowe Away

Fear and Longing in Los Angeles

Fright Nights, Big City

The Desmond Files

Evasion

Coversion (coming)

Sin Eater

Collateral Damage (Short Story)

I, Death

Short Story Collections

One Hand Screaming

Active Reader: And Other Cautionary Tales from the Book World

Snowman Shivers

Nocturnal Screams (8 Volumes)

Short Stories

A Murder of Scarecrows

Spirits

Anthologies (as Editor)

Campus Chills

Tesseracts Sixteen: Parnassus Unbound

Fiction River: Editor's Choice

Fiction River: Feel the Fear

Fiction River: Feel the Love

Fiction River: Superstitious

Obsessions

Pulp Fiction Issue #10

Non-Fiction / Paranormal / Ghost Stories

Haunted Hamilton

Spooky Sudbury

Tomes of Terror

Creepy Capital

Haunted Hospitals

Macabre Montreal

Too Macabre for Montreal

Watch for more at www.markleslie.ca.